SNOT-BOTS

RISE OF THE SNOT-BOTS

by John Sazaklis • illustrated by Shane Clester

STONE ARCH BOOKS
a capstone imprint

Published by Stone Arch Books, an imprint of Capstone
1710 Roe Crest Drive, North Mankato, Minnesota 56003
capstonepub.com

Library of Congress Cataloging-in-Publication Data
Names: Sazaklis, John, author. | Clester, Shane, illustrator.
Title: Rise of the snot-bots / by John Sazaklis ; illustrated by
    Shane Clester.
Description: North Mankato, Minnesota : Stone Arch Books, an
    imprint of Capstone, [2023] | Series: Snot-bots | Audience:
    Ages 8-11. | Audience: Grades 2-3.
Summary: Angry that the Clean Team was awarded the key to
    Electropolis, Sludge and his Snot-bots decide to crash the celebration
    party and muck the city up.
Identifiers: LCCN 2022025144 (print) | LCCN 2022025145 (ebook) |
    ISBN 9781666348897 (hardcover) | ISBN 9781666348842
    (paperback) | ISBN 9781666348859 (pdf) | ISBN 9781669021056
    (kindle edition)
Subjects: LCSH: Robots--Juvenile fiction. | Malicious mischief--
    Juvenile fiction. | Parties--Juvenile fiction. | Humorous stories. |
    CYAC: Robots--Fiction. | Cleanliness--Fiction. | Parties--Fiction. |
    Humorous stories. | LCGFT: Humorous fiction.
Classification: LCC PZ7.S27587 Ri 2023 (print) | LCC PZ7.S27587
    (ebook) | DDC 813.6 [E]--dc23/eng/20220726
LC record available at https://lccn.loc.gov/2022025144
LC ebook record available at https://lccn.loc.gov/2022025145

Editor: Aaron Sautter
Designer: Nathan Gassman
Production Specialist: Whitney Schaefer

Printed and bound in China.   PO#5449

TABLE OF CONTENTS

THE SNOT-BOTS

When an explosion at the Electropolis nuclear power plant leaks radiation into a nearby junkyard, the scrap metal inside turns into some messy mutations!

Rising from the slime and grime are—the Snot-Bots! The junkyard is their secret lair, the Fartress of Foulitude. These crude, rude robots are on a mission to muck things up!

SLUDGE

YUCK

MUCK

STINK + STUNK

The *Clean Team*

To combat the filthy foes of Electropolis, the city's citizens call upon their friends of freshness—the Clean Team!

Equipped with super-powered cleaning supplies, these high-tech heroes keep the city safe and sanitary . . . especially against nasty, no-good polluters like the Snot-Bots!

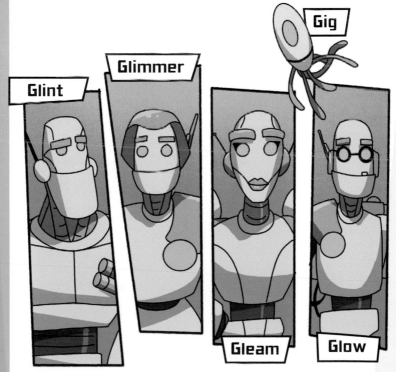

It's a special day in Electropolis.

"Let's hear it for the Clean Team!" shouts the mayor. "Their teamwork makes our city shimmer and shine!"

The crowd erupts in claps and cheers.

HOORAY!! WHOO-HOO!

The robot heroes high-five each other and take a bow.

"With us on the scene, our city will be **squeaky clean**!" Glint says. He is the leader of the Clean Team.

The mayor smiles and hands Glint the Key to the City.

Deep in the sewers, Sludge watches the ceremony from the Snot-Bots' Fartress.

"How **dare** they cheer for those squeaky-clean clods!" he yells.

Sludge spits a ball of thick, greasy slime at the screen.

PTOOEY! SPLAT!

"It's time to **yuck** things up!" he shouts.

"Right here, Boss!" says Yuck.

"No, I mean . . ." starts Sludge, eyes rolling. "Ugh, never mind. Just have the Snot-Bots report for duty."

"Will do, Boss! Hey, **duty** sounds like **doodie**! Ha!" Yuck snorts.

The bumbling bots barrel into the Fartress's command center.

CLANG! BANG! CLUNK! THUNK!

Yuck, Muck, Stink, and Stunk line up in front of Sludge.

"The mayor has done something **totally disgusting**," he says.

"Did she wash the dishes?" asks Stink.

"Did she brush her teeth?" asks Stunk.

"Worse!" answers Yuck. "She threw a party for the Clean Team!"

"We're going to crash that party!" says Sludge. "To the **Vomit Comet**!"

CHAPTER TWO:
PARTY POOPERS

FWOOOOSH!

The Vomit Comet blasts off from the Fartress and streaks across the sky.

It leaves behind a trail of thick, foul-smelling exhaust.

"We're coming up on
City Hall, boss," says Stink.

"You know what to do," orders
Sludge. "Let's rain on their party!"

Yuck and Muck roll over to the control panel. They pull a series of levers.

Gears grind and shift. Soon, a rusty hatch under the Vomit Comet opens up.

KRRRRRKKKK! CLANK!

In an instant, a gush of gooey, greasy oil splashes down below.

WHIRRRRRR! SPLOOOOSH!

The slimy muck **oozes** through the city's streets like lava. It taints everything it touches.

The city is in **complete chaos**! People start running everywhere.

"Yes! Scatter, you rotten little roaches!" Sludge laughs wickedly.

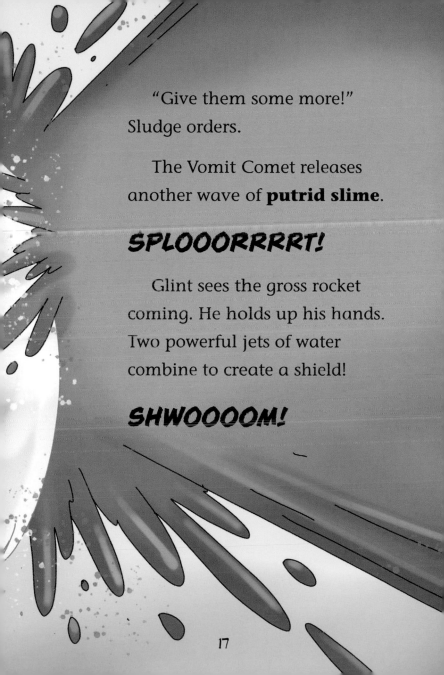

"Give them some more!" Sludge orders.

The Vomit Comet releases another wave of **putrid slime**.

SPLOOORRRRT!

Glint sees the gross rocket coming. He holds up his hands. Two powerful jets of water combine to create a shield!

SHWOOOOM!

CHAPTER THREE:
ROTTEN ROCKET

"Get those citizens to safety!" Glint commands.

The other heroes rush everyone into City Hall.

ZWIP! THWIP! ZOOM!

Once the people are safe, the Clean Team falls into formation with Glint. The team's all-purpose mini-bot pet, Gig, hovers above.

"The Snot-Bots are causing trashy trouble again," Gleam says. She is the second in command.

Bringing up the rear are the terrific twins, Glimmer and Glow. "We need to stop that sloppy **snot rocket**!" they say.

The Vomit Comet lands with a
thunderous **THUD!** in the town square.

"Activate the **Poop Chute**!" orders Sludge.

"Let 'er rip!" shout Stink and Stunk. The stinky brother bots gleefully press buttons on the control panel.

A slime-covered slide rolls out of the rocket's back end.

GRUUUNKKKK!

The Snot-Bots are ready to **funk** things up!

"Let's rumble until this dump is rubble!" Sludge shouts.

"Funny you should say that," says Glint. "Because the dump is exactly where *you're* going!

"Clean Team—**SHOWER POWER**!"

CHAPTER FOUR:

SLIME TIME

Glint and Gleam aim their power washers. A blast of bleach, hot water, and detergent covers Muck and Yuck.

Stink and Stunk quickly use their **Tag-Team Stank** move. Stink blows out a big belch. Meanwhile, Stunk lets a funky fart fly.

BLUUURP! BRRRRAT-TAT-TAT!

A toxic cloud of green gas fills the air.

The Clean Team is momentarily muddled by the Snot-Bots' foul fog.

"These rude dudes are **double trouble**!" Glimmer says.

"Let's show them what we can do," replies Glow.

The twins unite and let loose a super stream of sanitizer spray.

ZZZZZAAAAARK!

During the rock 'em, sock 'em rampage, Sludge spots a twinkling trinket.

"Hey, it's the Key to the City!" he crows. "Time for an upgrade! Now I can unlock my Superbot Snots!"

Sludge crams the key up his nose and gives it a twist.

CLANK!

CRANK!

YANK!

Then he pulls out the biggest, baddest, bot-booger ever!

CHAPTER FIVE:
SHOCKED BOTS

Sludge spins around and **flings** the super booger at the Clean Team guarding City Hall.

SPLOOOORCH!

The guardians of Electropolis are knocked off their feet. They're **trapped** by the sticky mix of slimy, crusty crud.

Sludge holds up the Key to the City in victory. The other Snot-Bots crowd around him.

"Welcome to Sludge City!" he cackles. "Time to learn a new slogan: Just say yes to the mess!"

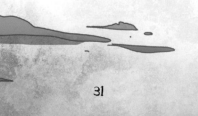

FWEEET!

Glint whistles for Gig. The whirly-bot dives down to the Clean Team's fearless leader.

"Gig, get me out. We have to stop those vile villains!" says Glint.

A high-speed buzzsaw pops out of Gig's chest. The bot begins to slice and dice.

BZZZZZZZZRT!

Seconds later, Glint is free! He sets his weapons to **Baking Soda Blast**. Then he covers the nasty cage with white, fizzy foam. The bubbling action soon breaks his team out of the super-snot trap.

CHIZ-OOOOM!

"Stop them!" Sludge yells. He holds the Key to the City high overhead.

Behind him is a buzzing electric fence. Glint sees this and smiles. "These Snot-Bots need a **shock** to their system!"

Together, the Clean Team blast Sludge with a powerful hot water shower.

SLOOOSH-A-SWOOOSH!

The steamy blast crashes into Sludge, and he hits the powered fence with a wet splash.

CRACK! ZZZRRK!

The other Snot-Bots rush in and try to pry the key from Sludge's hand. But they get zapped too!

ZZZZAAAP! CLUNK!

The conked-out bots **plop** into a pool of their own **slop**.

With the foul foes knocked out, the Clean Team gets to work. They use jet streams of soapy water to wash away the funky filth.

The mayor thanks the Clean Team for their service. She gives them a brand-new Key to the City.

"**Gross**!" growls Sludge, waking up. "Take us to jail so we don't have to watch this disgusting display!"

"Oh, you're going somewhere better," says Glint. "We're going to take you to the car wash!"

THE END

GLOSSARY

ceremony (SER-uh-moh-nee)—an activity performed to honor someone or mark a special occasion

chaos (KAY-os)—total confusion

command center (kuh-MAND SEN-tuhr)—a location where orders are given

detergent (dih-TUR-juhnt)—a soaplike substance used for cleaning

exhaust (eg-ZAWST)—the waste gases produced by an engine

formation (for-MAY-shuhn)—the way a group of people or objects is arranged

hatch (HACH)—a heavy door in a vehicle, such as a submarine or airplane

putrid (PYOO-trid)—rotten and stinking

sanitizer (SAN-ih-TIZE-uhr)—a substance used for cleaning and killing germs

slogan (SLOH-guhn)—a phrase or motto

trinket (TRING-kit)—a small ornament or piece of jewelry

TALK ABOUT IT

1. Have you ever had to clean up a big, smelly mess? What caused the mess, and how did you clean it?

2. If you could be a Snot-Bot, what kind would you be? What would be your super gross-out power, and how would you use it to fight the Clean Team?

WRITE ABOUT IT

3. At the start of the story, the Clean Team is given the Key to the City. Write a story describing what the Clean Team did to earn the reward.

4. If Gig wasn't able to help, how would Glint have gotten free from the super-snot trap? Write a new chapter explaining how Glint could free himself and his team.